Miyako from Tokyo

Hello, I am Miyako from Tokyo! Come inside to meet my family and my friends...

Miho Yamada
Illustrated by
Princesse Camcam

My name is Miyako. That means "pretty girl" in Japanese. I am eight years old. I live in Tokyo, the capital of Japan. Tokyo is a huge city with lots of towers and buildings everywhere. The red and white tower is the Tokyo Tawā. It is more than 1,000 feet (300 meters) high. The big park on the right is Kokyo Gaien. That's where the Imperial Palace is and where the Emperor and his family live. There are also the wonderful Meiji and Yasukuni shrines with their beautiful trees and temples.

Tokyo is a very modern city filled with technology, but you can also find more traditional neighborhoods. Here you can see the Ueno/Asakusa neighborhood that isn't far from where I live. I love to walk there with my girlfriends because it's very lively. There are lots of modern department stores and small food carts that sell hot food: soups, yakisoba (sautéed noodles), takoyaki (octopus dumplings), and okonomiyaki (savory stuffed pancakes). Yum!

Here's the big Ueno Park that has the oldest zoo in Japan. I sometimes go there after school with my little brother, Masashi. My favorite animals are the pandas and the elephants. Last year, my class was chosen to welcome two new elephants. I was the one who gave them the basket of fruits, but one of the elephants got a little cheeky.

I live near the zoo. My house is made of concrete, but it looks like wood. Don't forget to take your shoes off before you come in! Look at the beautiful sliding doors! They're made of washi paper. That's a traditional, handmade Japanese paper made from natural fibers. Our house is divided in two parts: one part for my parents, my brother and I, and the other part for my grandparents. Sometimes, my grandmother plays the koto, a traditional Japanese musical instrument. I love to listen to her play while I serve the tea.

My mom's name is Yoshiko. She teaches Japanese calligraphy. I've already taken some lessons with her students. Preparing the ink and directing the brush is very important. It's still a little hard for me, but I like it a lot. I love the smell of the ink. My dad, Hiroshi, is a conductor for the Shinkansen, a high-speed train. I've taken it many times to Osaka and Kyoto.

In the morning, I walk to school with children in my neighborhood. The oldest child is in charge of keeping count of the children. School finishes at 3:30. On our way home, the merchants always ask us how our day was. Sometimes, they even give us candy! We often stop at the book store to buy comic books. Do you read comic books?

My teacher's name is Mr. Kumano. He wears very funny glasses! When he comes into the classroom, everybody has to get up and greet him by saying "Good Morning" In my school, all the boys wear shorts and they carry black book bags. We girls carry red book bags. We all wear yellow hats to go to school and go home.

At recess, I meet up with my boyfriends, Takuya and Satoru and my girlfriends, Yuri and Asako. We're always together and the boys jump rope with us! In the fall, the children have to pick up the dead leaves in the courtyard. In fact, in Japan every school participates in household tasks. Last week it was my group's turn to clean the classroom.

17

I do kendo, a Japanese martial art. I go every Saturday afternoon with my friend, Asako. To intimidate your opponent, you have to really concentrate before doing the kiai, a special scream that frees your energy. Asako's big brother is a Sumō champion. He's really strong! My dad took us one day to see him in a tournament in Ryōgoku Kokugikan, the Sumō arena in Tokyo. It was really amazing and lots of fun!

In Japan, we eat with chopsticks. At home, we eat on my grandparents' tatamis (floor mat). That's more fun! My mom makes lots of good food. I love sushi and sashimi, tonkatsu, which is breaded pork, and nikujyaga, a dish made with meat and potatoes. My father makes gyōza, which is Japanese ravioli. Have you ever eaten that?

In my country, we have lots of festivals for every season. My favorite festival is Momo-no-sekku, the girls' festival. We display our dolls dressed in traditional costumes at home. Afterwards, we eat hina-arare, colorful sweet rice cakes.

In May, it's the boys' turn for a festival! For Tango-no-sekku, bright-colored carps made of canvas are tied to masts taller than the houses. We eat kashiwa-mochi, a chilled rice paste stuffed with kidney beans.

For our summer vacation in July, we go to my Uncle Takayuki and Aunt Hiroko's house. They live in a beautiful house near Lake Ashi, 60 miles (100 kilometers) from Tokyo. On the lake, you can take a pirate ship and marvel at "Fujisan", Mount Fuji, the highest peak in Japan. It's an amazing volcano with a totally white peak. When they were young, my parents climbed all the way to its crater.

In Japan, New Year's is a big family holiday that is called Oshogatsu. To celebrate, we make osechi, the traditional Japanese meal. On New Year's Eve, we eat buckwheat noodles. Then we put on our kimonos and go to the temple to worship and bring good luck for the New Year!

That's it! The tour is over! !
I hope to see you soon
in Tokyo. Goodbye!

Miyako's Little Japanese-French-English Phrasebook

- こんにちは。**Konnichiwa !** Bonjour ! Hello!
- わたしの　なまえは　みやこです。**Watashi no namae wa Miyako desu.** Je m'appelle Miyako. My name is Miyako.
- はっさいです。**Hassai desu.** J'ai huit ans. I'm eight years old.
- とうきょうに　すんでいます。**Tokyo ni sunde imasu.** J'habite à Tokyo. I live in Tokyo.
- どこに　すんでいますか? **Doko ni sunde imasuka ?** Où habites-tu? Where do you live?
- おとうとが　ひとり　います。**Otōto ga hitori imasu.** J'ai un frère. I have one brother.
- きょうだいが　いますか。**Kyōdai ga imasuka ?** As-tu des frères et soeurs ? Do you have any brothers or sisters?
- おすしが　だいすきです。**Osushi ga daisuki desu.** J'adore les sushi. I love sushi.
- おしゅうじが　すきです。**Oshūji ga suki desu.** J'aime la calligraphie japonaise. I love Japanese calligraphy.
- きものを　きるのが　すきです。**Kimono o kiru no ga sukidesu.** J'aime porter mon kimono. I love wearing my kimono.
- うたを　うたうのは　すきですか。**Uta o utau no wa suki desuka ?** Aimes tu chanter ? Do you like to sing?
- さようなら、またね! **Sayōnara, Matane !** Au revoir, salut ! Goodbye, Cheers!

30

• とうきょう　タワー
Tokyo Tawā
Tower of Tokyo

• こと **Koto**
Japanese string
instrument

• しんかんせん **Shinkansen**
Japanese high-speed train

• けんどう **Kendō**
Modern Japanese
martial art

• すもう **Sumō**
Japanese wrestling

• すし **Sushi** • さしみ **Sashimi**
Sushi : rice dish combined
with fish and vegetables
Sashimi: slices of raw fish

• ふじさん **Fujisan**
Mount Fuji

• まんが **Mang**
Japanese
comic strip

Your AV² Media Enhanced book gives you a fiction readalong online.
Log on to www.av2books.com and enter the unique book code from
page 2 to use your readalong.

AV² Readalong Navigation

HIGHLIGHTED
TEXT

HOME

CLOSE

START
READING

READ

TITLE
INFORMATION

INFO

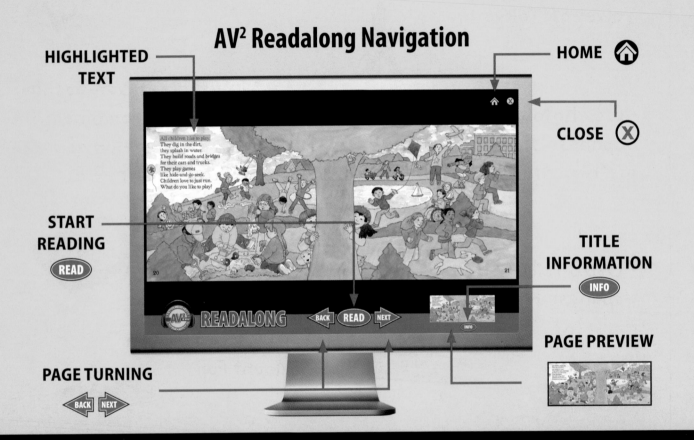

PAGE TURNING

BACK NEXT

PAGE PREVIEW

Published by AV² by Weigl
350 5ᵗʰ Avenue, 59ᵗʰ Floor New York, NY 10118
Websites: www.av2books.com   www.weigl.com

ABC MELODY Éditions
26, rue Liancourt 75014
Paris, France

Printed in the United States of America in North Mankato, Minnesota
1 2 3 4 5 6 7 8 9 0 18 17 16 15 14

042014
WEP080414

Library of Congress Control Number: 2014937156

ISBN 978-1-4896-2268-6 (hardcover)
ISBN 978-1-4896-2269-3 (single user eBook)
ISBN 978-1-4896-2270-9 (multi-user eBook)